S0-CMQ-021

Little Boys Bible

Christmas Storybook

Little Boys Bible Christmas Storybook

Published by New Kids Media™ in association with Baker Book House Company, Grand Rapids, Michigan.

ISBN 0-8010-4462-6

Printed in the United States of America.

1 2 3 4 5 6 7 — 03 02 01 00

Carolyn Larsen
Illustrated by Caron Turk

Published in association with

Read My Lips!

"You look like you saw a ghost," a friend said to Zechariah. "Not a ghost—an angel," Zechariah screamed . . . well, he wanted to scream, but when he opened his mouth nothing came out but air! God took away his voice because he didn't believe the angel's message.

Zechariah finished his work at the temple and hurried home to his wife, Elizabeth. He had something important to tell her—if he could make her understand.

"Are you crazy?" Elizabeth had never seen her husband like this. As a priest, Zechariah was normally quiet and kind of stuffy. But here he was jumping around, waving his arms and trying to speak, but no sound came out. "You have something to tell me, right? Just say it!" Elizabeth was frustrated . . . so was Zechariah. Finally, he grabbed her broom and scratched something in the dirt with the handle. He stepped aside so Elizabeth could read, "We're going to have a baby."

"Now I know you're crazy. You know how old I am. Do you seriously think a baby could grow in this shriveled old body?" Elizabeth grabbed her broom and started back to the house. But when she glanced back at Zechariah's face, she stopped. "You're serious aren't you?" Suddenly her knees felt weak. She had to sit down. "A baby," she thought. "After all these years I'm going to have a baby!"

The next few months were spent getting ready for the blessed event—Zechariah built a cradle, Elizabeth knitted booties. "Come quick!" she would call to Zechariah and he would run to put his hands on her growing tummy and feel their son kick. Sometimes he got frustrated that he couldn't tell his wife how excited he felt about the birth of their child—the special child who would grow up to tell the world that the Messiah was coming!

When their precious baby boy was born all of Zechariah and Elizabeth's relatives came to help them celebrate. Everyone had an opinion of what the baby's name should be. In the middle of the shouting, Zechariah took a tablet and scratched HIS NAME IS JOHN and held it up for all to see. (That's what the angel had said to name him.) Immediately Zechariah's voice came back and he and Elizabeth praised God together!

Based on Luke 1:5-25, 57-64

Becoming a Man of God

A man of God is sometimes quiet.

Zechariah was alone in the temple doing his work as a priest, so it was probably quiet. When he didn't believe the angel's message and God took his voice away it was definitely quiet.

It's very hard to hear God speak, or anyone else for that matter, if you are always making noise.

Do people ever tell you to "Calm down!" or "Use your inside voice!" Why do you think that happens? When someone is trying to explain something to you, do you listen quietly?

A Mom's Touch

More than likely being quiet is not one of your little guy's strong points since most little boys like to make noise. Talk about what he might miss if he isn't sometimes quiet.

Share a story of a time when you didn't listen quietly and you missed some instructions or information. What happened?

If your son does listen quietly tell him how much you appreciate that. Then, go outside together and sit quietly. Listen to all the sounds around you.

Remind your son that God sometimes speaks in a whisper that we hear inside our hearts. If we're always noisy, we might miss what he's saying to us.

A Verse to Remember

Be silent and know that I am God.

Psalm 46:10

A Trusting Step Dad

"Joseph, God knows you are confused and scared. That's OK. He wants you to know that Mary was telling you the truth. The baby she's going to have is the Son of God." Joseph wiggled in his sleep. He didn't usually dream about bigger-than-life shiny white angels—and yet here was one in his dream . . . a big one . . . and it was speaking to him!

"Oooohhh!" Mary moaned when the donkey stumbled on a stone in the road.

"Are you OK, Mary?" Joseph felt so bad that Mary was bouncing around on the bumpy donkey. She could have stayed home while he went to Bethlehem for the census, but her baby could be born any day and she didn't want to be away from him. "We'll be there soon. Then we'll get a nice hotel room and you can rest," Joseph promised his very pregnant wife.

"I don't feel so good," Mary moaned. Joseph had to admit that the smell of sweaty bodies and dirty animals crowding the streets was sickening.

"Hang on, I'll run in and get a room," Joseph promised, hurrying into the inn. In a few minutes he was back. "It's full. There aren't any rooms left in all of Bethlehem. The best we can get is a spot in the stable. I'm so sorry, Mary." But Mary didn't even care—she just wanted to get off that donkey!

Joseph pulled clean hay from the loft and made a bed for Mary to lie on. She fell asleep right away, even with the cows mooing and the donkey braying. Sometime later she shook Joseph awake, "The baby! The baby is coming!" Poor Joseph wasn't sure what to do, but Mary was so frightened that she didn't want him to leave her to find a midwife. The animals seemed to sense that something special was happening. They were very quiet when Joseph placed the baby boy in Mary's exhausted arms.

In the dim light of dawn Joseph looked up to see some scraggly shepherds peeking over the stable door. "An angel told us that your baby is the Messiah. We came to worship him." It seemed to Joseph that Mary wasn't even surprised by what they said. Then he remembered the words of the angel in his dream. "This child will save his people from their sins."

"It's true," he thought. "The angel's words were true!"

Based on Matthew 1:20-25; Luke 2:1-20

Becoming a Man of God

A man of God trusts God plan.

Joseph and Mary had been planning their wedding for quite a while. All their plans were made and Joseph didn't expect any surprises. But, God had other plans. The news that Mary was expecting a baby was definitely not in their plans. Joseph trusted God enough to continue with the wedding and see what happened.

Have you ever walked into a room that was completely dark? You can't even see your hand in front of your face, let alone where you're walking and whether or not you're going to trip over something? That may be kind of how Joseph felt. He was willing to keep going, even though he didn't really know what was ahead for him.

A Mom's Touch

Share an example of trust from your childhood. Perhaps you had to move to a new town and you had to trust your parents' judgment that everything would be OK. Tell your son how you felt when all you could do was trust someone else—there was nothing you could do yourself about the situation.

Ask your son when he has felt that all he could do in a situation was trust someone else to handle it. Was he afraid? How did it turn out? Build his confidence in God by talking about how he has come through in every situation. Reinforce that God is worthy of our trust because he loves us.

A Verse to Remember

Trust in the LORD with all your heart; do not depend on your own understanding.

Proverbs 3:5

Sometimes Joseph nearly forgot that Jesus wasn't a boy like every other boy. He laughed, slept, burped, spit up, just like any other little one. But the truth slammed into Joseph's heart the day some wise men from another country showed up on fancy camels with colorful blankets on them. They brought fancy gifts to Jesus and worshiped him. Joseph noticed that Mary was taking everything in, but not saying a word as she cradled Jesus in her arms. "I wonder what is ahead for this little guy," he thought.

A few days after the wise men left the angel visited Joseph's dream again. "Get your little family out of town! Quick! King Herod wants to kill Jesus!" Joseph felt his heart leap into his throat. His stomach hurt and a cold sweat broke out on his forehead. "God is trusting us to raise his son," he thought. "I can't let Herod hurt him!"

"Mary, get up. Dress the baby. We have to leave town now," Joseph called. Mary got up and began to pack a few things before she woke the baby. "No! We don't have time to pack. We must hurry. Jesus' life is in danger!" That got Mary moving. In just a few moments she was on the donkey with Jesus sleeping in her arms. Joseph walked ahead of them and the little family disappeared into the darkness outside of Bethlehem.

Joseph, Mary, and Jesus settled in Egypt. "I wonder how long we'll be here," Mary wondered. It was hard to live in a foreign land where the people spoke a different language and their customs were different. The Egyptians didn't even worship God.

Finally, one night the angel came back to Joseph's dream. "King Herod is dead," the angel said. "It's safe to take Jesus home now."

Joseph and Mary were so happy to be able to go home. They quickly packed the few things they had accumulated in Egypt. Instead of returning to Bethlehem, the little family went home to Nazareth. It was so good to see family and friends again! "Momma, Poppa, I've missed you so much. This is our son, Jesus!" Mary cried. Finally, Mary and Joseph could introduce Jesus to their family! It was good to be home.

Based on Matthew 2:1-23

Becoming a Man of God

A man of God protects.

Joseph could have refused to run to Egypt. He could have said that he would stay in Bethlehem and fight for Jesus' safety. But Joseph was smart enough to know that he should follow any instructions an angel gave him because the most important thing was to protect Jesus from King Herod.

When has your mom or dad protected you? It's a nice feeling to know that someone is keeping you safe, isn't it?

A Mom's Touch

When your children are small you spend a lot of time protecting them from the dangers they don't understand. Share a time when you remember protecting your son. Tell him how very much you love him and how glad you are that he is safe and healthy.

Ask your son if he understands that the rules you make for him are usually for his protection. Talk about ways your son can protect others—a younger sibling or a pet—ways he can show responsibility. Talk about some of God's rules and how they are for our protection. Thank him for his protection.

A Verse to Remember

The LORD keeps watch over you as you come and go, both now and forever.

Psalm 121:8

A Child Shall Lead Them

"I'm so excited!" Jesus could barely sit down to dinner. "I love going to Jerusalem for the Passover Festival. Can I walk with my friends, huh, can I?"

"Hmm, I think you're old enough to walk with your friends this year," Mary smiled. "But sit down and eat dinner now. We still have lots to do before we leave tomorrow morning." Jesus obeyed his mother, as he always did, but it was all he could do to sit still and finish dinner.

Early the next morning Jesus was dressed and waiting at the door when his parents got up. Soon they were in the middle of the crowd walking to Jerusalem. "Jesus, over here!" someone called. He ran to join his friends and they laughed and played games as they walked. The Passover celebration was wonderful! Jesus and the other children were quiet and respectful as they and their parents thanked God for taking care of his people.

When the festival ended the tired worshipers headed home. "Have you seen Jesus?" Mary asked.

"No, he's probably with his friends," Joseph answered.

A while later one of Jesus' friends came up. "Where's Jesus?" he asked.

"We thought he was with you," Mary answered.

"No, none of the guys have seen him all day." A stab of fear sank deep into Mary's heart as she shouted, "Jesus is lost!"

Mary grabbed Joseph's hand and they ran back to Jerusalem. They ran until their sides hurt and their breath came in short gasps so strong that they couldn't speak. "He's only twelve. What will happen to him in the big city? How could we lose him?" Mary's panicked heart cried.

For three long days Mary and Joseph searched the city, up and down the streets, every nook and cranny, everywhere they could think to look! Jesus was nowhere to be found!

They had nearly given up when they heard someone mention a boy who was teaching the temple teachers about God. Immediately, Mary and Joseph ran to the temple. It was Jesus! "Do you know what we've been through? We've looked everywhere for you," Mary cried.

Jesus calmly answered, "Didn't you know that I would be in my father's house?" Then he went home with Mary and Joseph. She was so relieved that he was OK that she couldn't stop touching his arm or ruffling his hair.

Based on Luke 2:41-52

Becoming a Man of God

A man of God never gives up.

Imagine the panic Mary and Joseph must have felt. God trusted them to take care of his son . . . and they lost him! Immediately Mary and Joseph began searching for Jesus. They looked for one day and they didn't find him, then they looked for another day but they didn't find him. But, Mary and Joseph didn't give up—they kept looking and looking until they found Jesus.

The best things in life take hard work to achieve. Have you ever worked really hard to learn something? Maybe you wanted to give up in the middle, but you didn't, you kept trying and trying until you learned it. Did you feel like celebrating when you finally learned what you had been working on?

A Mom's Touch

Share a story with your son detailing your own perseverance. Tell him about something you had to work constantly to achieve or learn. Let him know how you struggled with it, maybe wanting to give up, but you kept on going.

Remember when you were a child? Big projects or long-term projects sometimes were overwhelming. It was hard to stick with something until it was finished. If you have seen your son stick with a project to completion, compliment him on that perseverance. Talk about areas where he might need to work on sticking with a project. Help him make a plan to do so.

A Verse to Remember

Hold on to the pattern of right teaching you have learned from me. And remember to live in the faith and love that you have in Christ Jesus.

2 Timothy 1:13